D0716384

This edition produced for The Book People Ltd, Hall Wood Avenue,
Haydock, St Helens, WA11 9UL

First published in hardback in Great Britain by HarperCollins Publishers Ltd in 1995
First published in Picture Lions in 1999
3 5 7 9 10 8 6 4
ISBN: 0 00 762734 3

Picture Lions is an imprint of the Children's Division, part of HarperCollins Publishers Ltd

Text and illustrations copyright © Nick Butterworth 1995
The author asserts the moral right to be identified as the author of the work

A CIP catalogue record for this title is available from the British Library.
All rights reserved. No part of this publication may be reproduced, stored in a retrieval system or transmitted in any form or by any means, electronic, mechanical, photocopying, recording or otherwise, without the prior permission of HarperCollins Publishers Ltd, 77-85 Fulham Palace Road, Hammersmith, London W6 8JB.

The HarperCollins website address is www.**fire**and**water**.com

Manufactured in China

THE CROSS RABBIT

NICK BUTTERWORTH

TED SMART

It was a bright, cold winter's day.

Snow had fallen in the night and now everything in the park had been turned into a guessing game.

"It looks wonderful," said Percy the park keeper, "but it makes a lot of work."

Standing next to Percy was a rather old and cross-looking rabbit.

"Well, quite so," said the rabbit. "But now, what about these mice? They're making a dreadful nuisance of themselves."

Percy found it hard not to laugh when he saw what was making the rabbit so cross.

The mice were having great fun.

Percy began to chuckle, but quickly turned the chuckle into a cough. After all, this was no fun for an old rabbit who only wanted to curl up and sleep through the cold weather.

"Now come along, you mice," said Percy. "You must go and play somewhere else. And," he added, "try to stay out of mischief."

The mice looked very disappointed. Slowly they walked away, dragging their toboggans behind them.

The old rabbit said thank you to Percy and then disappeared into his burrow.

Percy got on with clearing the snow. It was hot work even in the cold weather. First he took off his cap. Then his scarf. And then, even his gloves.

Percy worked hard all morning.

He mopped his brow again and looked at his work.

"Very good," he said to himself. "I think I deserve a spot of lunch."

Percy reached for his bag and pulled out a flask.

"That's funny," he said. "I'm sure I put the cup on the top this morning."

"I know, I'll have my yogurt first and drink from the empty carton."

Percy took out a strawberry yogurt and began to rummage through his bag.

"That's odd," he said. "No spoon. Hmm."

It was a strange lunch. A lid was missing from a small box of dates and the bottom half of one of Percy's cheese rolls had disappeared. And Percy was sure he had packed an orange but there was no sign of it now. It was all very puzzling.

It felt colder to Percy as he went back to work. He reached for his scarf and his cap, but now they had disappeared too!

"This is most peculiar," said Percy.

Then, as he gazed around looking for his cap and scarf, Percy was amazed to see his gloves walking off by themselves!

"I must be dreaming," said Percy.

"I'd like to be dreaming," said a cross voice. It was the old rabbit again. "Those mice are making a terrible noise. Would you speak to them please?" And with that the rabbit stumped off.

Percy followed.

"Look!" said the rabbit.

Percy looked. The mice had been very busy indeed! And they were having a marvellous time.

"Hello Percy!" they called. But suddenly they looked worried. "You're not going to tell us to stop, are you?"

Percy glanced at the old rabbit.

"Well . . . no," he said to the mice. "We just wondered if you could have a marvellous time a little more quietly?"

The mice cheered.

"We'll try!" they squeaked loudly.

"Come on," said Percy to the rabbit. "I think I've got some cotton wool in my bag. A little in each ear should do the trick."

NICK BUTTERWORTH was born in North London in 1946 and grew up in a sweet shop in Essex. He now lives in Suffolk with his wife Annette and their two children, Ben and Amanda.

The inspiration for the Percy the Park Keeper books came from Nick Butterworth's many walks through the local park with the family dog, Jake. The stories have sold over two million copies and are loved by children all around the world. Their popularity has led to the making of a stunning animated television series, now available on video from HIT Entertainment plc.

Read all the stories about Percy and his animal friends. . .

then enjoy the Percy activity books.

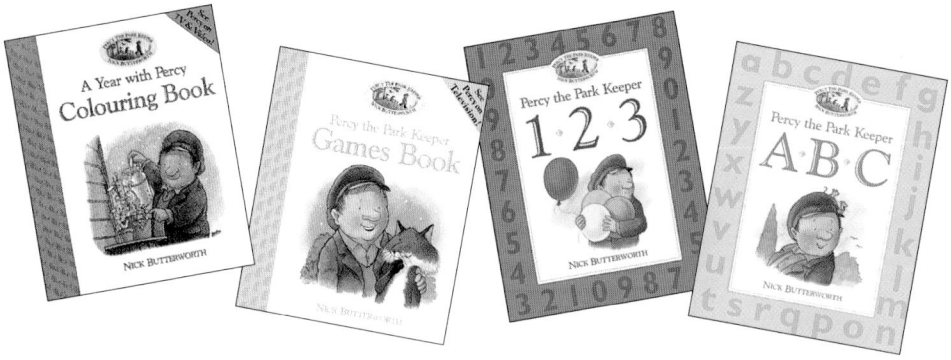

And don't forget you can now see Percy on video too!